Santa Mouse Stories

By MICHAEL BROWN

Sandy Creek
NEW YORK

Table of Contents

Santa Mouse

By MICHAEL BROWN

Illustrated by ELFRIEDA DEWITT

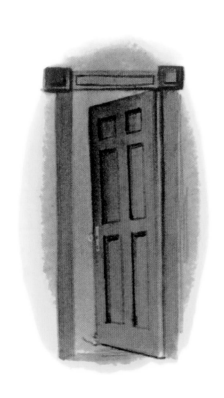

Once there was a little mouse
who didn't have a name.

He lived in a great big house, this mouse,
the only mouse in the whole, wide house.

He used to play a game.

He'd daydream
        he had playmates

who were friendly
        as could be.

While some of them
        would bring their dolls

and dress up
        and have tea,

There were
others who'd
play cowboys

or be Eskimos

or Spanish.

But when he'd try
  to touch them,

like a bubble,
  they would vanish.

Now, through the year,
    this little mouse

had saved one
    special thing:

A piece of cheese!

The kind that makes an angel want to sing.

On Christmas Eve, he brushed his teeth,

and as he washed his paws,

He thought, "My goodness, no one gives
a gift to Santa Claus!"

He ran to get his pretty cheese,
and after he had found it,

the paper from some chewing gum
he quickly wrapped around it.

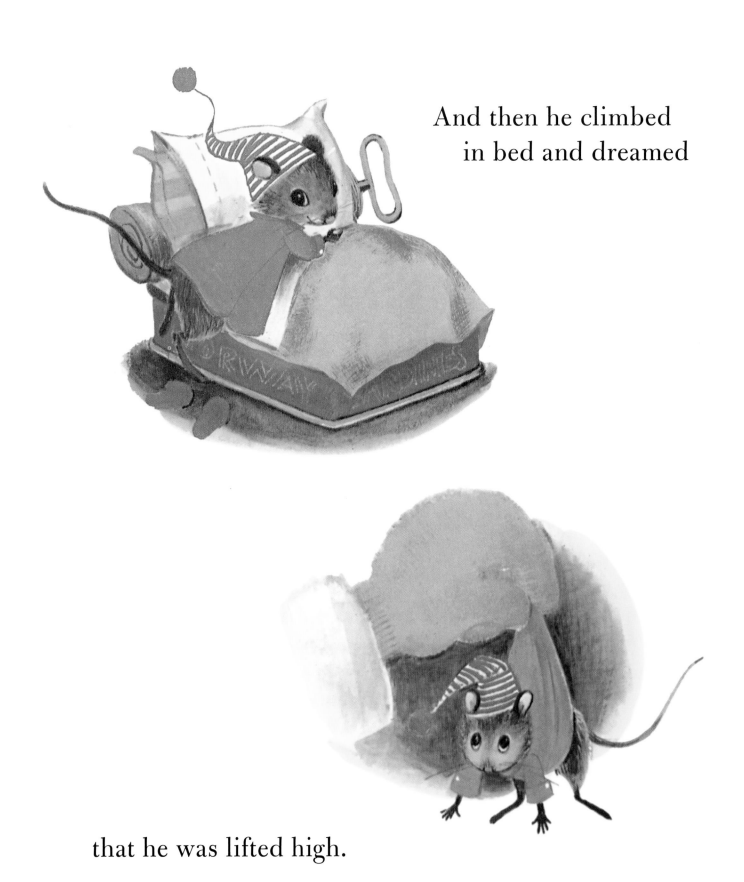

And then he climbed
in bed and dreamed

that he was lifted high.

He woke to find that he was looking
right in Santa's eye!

"I thank you for my gift,"
said Santa.

"Tell me, what's your name?"

"I haven't any," said the mouse.

"You haven't? That's a shame!

"You know, I need a helper
as I travel house to house,
and I shall give a name to you:

I'll call you Santa Mouse.

"So here's your beard,

and here's your suit,

and here's each shiny,

tiny

boot.

"You mustn't sneeze, and don't you cough.

Just put them on, and we'll be off!"

Then over all the rooftops,
on a journey with no end,
away they went together,
Santa with his tiny friend.

And so, this Christmas, if you please,
beneath the tree that's in your house,

Why don't you leave
a piece of cheese?

You know who'll thank you?

Santa Mouse!

Can you find Santa Mouse in this drawing?

Santa Mouse, Where Are You?

By MICHAEL BROWN

Illustrated by ELFRIEDA DEWITT

Ev'ry year, when it's December,
we're excited as can be,
for that's when we remember
it is time to get a tree.

We don't want a tree too tiny
or too tall to fit the house;
the tree we want has got to be
just right for Santa Mouse.

Santa Mouse is Santa's helper.

He goes with him ev'ry year,
and it really isn't Christmas

unless both of them appear.

Santa brings big presents in
that come for you and me,
while Santa Mouse takes tiny gifts
and climbs up in the tree.

He puts them right next to the trunk
or way out on a limb.
(If a gift is in the branches,
then we know it came from him!)

Now, once upon a time, someone
who looked a lot like you
was putting lights upon a tree,
some green, some red, some blue.

When suddenly this person said,
"You know what there should be?
A light right at the very top,
so Santa Mouse can see!"

It took a little help, of course,
to set that special light,
but finally, when bedtime came,
it looked exactly right.

Away up high, above the rest,
it shed a gentle beam,
and when little eyes grew sleepy,
it was shining in a dream.

Now, far off, in his workshop,
Santa Mouse was wrapping toys.
He was hurrying to finish
lots of things for girls and boys.

As he hunted for a ribbon,
suddenly this happy fellow
gave a whistle of surprise,
because he found one that was yellow.

He had needed something special
for a very special present,

but then a voice called him,
very deep, yet very pleasant …

"It's time to travel, Santa Mouse!
You know we can't be late!"
And Santa stepped into his sleigh,
"Come on, the deer won't wait!"

So Santa Mouse came running
with his present at his side,
and he leaped for Santa's shoulder—
it was time for them to ride.

Off they flew, as fast as lightning—
Santa Mouse was holding on.
But he felt his gift was slipping,
then, my goodness, it was gone!

He said, "Stop!" and tried to save it;
at that moment, off he fell.
But old Santa didn't know it,
and the sleigh went on pell-mell.

He was falling, calling, "Santa!"
But with darkness all around,
there was no one there to hear him—
he was headed for the ground!

Till he thought what he was holding,
tucked his whiskers in his suit,
took the paper and the ribbon
and produced a parachute!

Then KERPLUNK! he hit a snowbank
and disappeared from sight,

But he crawled out with his gift
and looked around him in the night.

What he thought was, "I am lost—
everything is cold and bare.
The thing to do is find a house
and wait for Santa there."

But he found nothing but the wind
that chilled him through and through.
It seemed to whisper, "Santa Mouse,
where ARE you, where are YOU?"

"Here I am!" he shouted bravely
as he trudged on through the storm,
holding tightly to his present
as if that could keep him warm.

He sat down and with a sniffle
tied the ribbon in a bow.
Then he noticed something funny—
on the bow there was a glow.

Somewhere near, a light was shining!
He jumped up, and it was true,
for a tiny, golden glimmering
was gleaming through the blue.

Remember how one special light
was placed for Santa Mouse?
He could see it now—it lit the way
for him to reach the house.

He crept inside, and climbed up high
to place it in the tree,
then went to sleep to wait
for Santa Claus, like you and me.

And that's where Santa found him
late that night upon his way.
He picked him up and kissed him
and then tucked him in his sleigh.

So this year, when it is Christmas
and you decorate your tree,
why not put one light upon it
that's as high up as can be?

You may find a tiny present
Christmas morning in your house.
If it's tied with yellow ribbon,
then who brought it?

Santa Mouse!

MR. SQUIRREL

Santa Mouse Meets Montague

By MICHAEL BROWN

Illustrated by GEORGE DESANTIS

Montague Mouse was a mean little thing
who often behaved like a rat.
He did things that weren't nice,
like scaring young mice
by hollering, "Here comes a cat!"

His mother stayed busy—she ran Mouse Hotel
up high in an attic, all hidden away
in a cupboard with doors,

where she polished the floors
and she cooked

and she washed
and she cleaned
every day.

What Santa Claus had heard about him
he could not believe,
and so he said to Santa Mouse,
"Tomorrow's Christmas Eve.
Take off your suit and pack a bag.
Go down and ring the bell
and have a look at Montague,
who lives at Mouse Hotel."

So Santa Mouse packed up his things
(he packed a piece of cheese as well),
and off he went on Christmas Eve
to check in there at Mouse Hotel.

He left his luggage by the bed,
washed up and then went down to dine,

and that's when Montague crept up
and entered Number 29!

He tiptoed in—he looked around,

he opened the suitcase that he found,

and there inside he saw a suit,

complete with hat

and beard

and boot.

"What fun!" he thought. "I'll get dressed up,
and I know what I'll do!"
But what he did when he put them on
is sad to tell to you.

He looked into the kitchen,
and his mother wasn't there,

so he called his little sisters,
who came scrambling down the stair.

When they saw him, what they did
was burst into applause,
because they thought on Christmas Eve
that he was Santa Claus.

Then Montague pulled off the beard
and laughed and said, "You see,
there ISN'T any Santa Claus!
Ha, ha! It's only me!"

THEN...

A door flew open in that house,
and there stood angry Santa Mouse.
He said, "You KNOW that's wrong to do!
Just wait till I get through with you!"

He started after Montague,
the little mice began to yell,

and pots

and pans

and apples

and

potatoes flew pell-mell!

The chase was on, with cups and saucers
smashing, crashing from the shelf,
till all at once, someone cried,

"STOP!"

And there stood Santa Claus himself.

"You mice have made a mess," he said,
and looked at them and shook his head.
"You've got to clean it up, you two,
and while you do, I'll speak to you.

"Now, Montague, you told these mice
I wasn't real, which wasn't nice.

"And Santa Mouse, you had a fit—
you lost your temper, you'll admit.

"And yet, you know, there's nothing wrong
with being angry not as long

As you just SAY it and don't hit,
for no one wants that, not a bit."

And then he picked up Santa Mouse
and whispered something very low.
Quite suddenly they disappeared—
on Christmas Eve they work, you know.

And Montague looked at his mother.
In his eye there came a tear.
"Sorry, Mom," he said. He knew
that he would get no gift this year.

But he was wrong, for in the morning,
labeled with a big red pen,
a box stood there with his name on it.
Santa had come back again!

He opened it, and there appeared
(with cap and belt and boots and beard)
a suit that Santa Mouse had sewn
for Montague to call his own.

The card inside said, "Let's be friends,"
and that is how this story ends,
as Montague held in his paws
the proof there IS a Santa Claus.

Santa is a friend who's true,
and I believe in him.

Don't you?